KINGFISHER
a Houghton Mifflin Company imprint
222 Berkeley Street
Boston, Massachusetts 02116
www.houghtonmifflinbooks.com

First published in 2005
2 4 6 8 10 9 7 5 3 1

LIBRARY OF CONGRESS CATALOGING-IN-PUBLICATION DATA
has been applied for.

ISBN 0-7534-5849-7
ISBN 978-07534-5849-5

Printed in India
1TR/0605/THOM/PICA(PICA)09WFO/C

HO, HO, HO!

150 HYSTERICAL CHRISTMAS JOKES

KINGFISHER

BOSTON

What Christmas carol do parents like?
"Silent Night."

Why does Santa have three gardens?
So he can hoe, hoe, hoe!

Knock, knock.
Who's there?
Hanna.
Hanna who?
Hanna partridge in a pear tree!

Where do you find elves?
Depends on where you left them!

What is green, covered in tinsel, and says "Ribbet, ribbet"?
A mistle-toad.

What's the best key to get for Christmas?
A turkey!

**What did
Mrs. Claus say
to Santa Claus?**
*"It looks like
rain, dear."*

**What squeaks
and is scary?**
*The Ghost of
Christmouse Past!*

**What does Frosty
the Snowman wear
on his head?**
An ice cap.

**Who brings Christmas
presents to police
stations?**
Santa Clues.

**Why did the
reindeer wear
black boots?**
*Because its brown
ones were all muddy.*

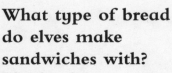

**What type of bread
do elves make
sandwiches with?**
Shortbread!

What happens when Frosty the Snowman gets dandruff?
He gets snowflakes.

Who brings Christmas presents to baby sharks?
Santa Jaws.

Who is never hungry on Christmas?
The turkey—it's always stuffed.

How many elves does it take to change a lightbulb?
Ten. One to change the bulb and nine to stand on each other's shoulders.

How do chihuahuas say "Merry Christmas"?
Fleas Navidog!

Why didn't Santa Claus get wet when he lost his umbrella?
It wasn't raining.

Teacher: Can anyone name Santa's reindeer?

Anne: Dasher, Dancer, Prancer, Vixen, Comet, Cupid,
Donner, Blitzen, Rudolph, and Al.

Teacher: Are you sure about Al?

Anne: Yes— "Then Al the reindeer loved him . . ."

**What does Frosty the
Snowman's wife
put on her face
at night?**
Cold cream.

Santa travels in
a sleigh. What do
elves travel in?
Minivans!

Waiter, waiter, my
turkey has gone off!
Which way did it go?

One Christmas a teacher who hated giving homework, a nice babysitter, and Santa Claus were riding in the elevator of a very expensive hotel. Just before the doors opened, they all noticed a ten-dollar bill lying on the floor. Which one picked it up?

Santa Claus, of course, because the other two don't exist!

Why are Christmas trees like bad knitters?
They both drop their needles!

What do reindeer always say before telling you a joke?
"This one will sleigh you!"

Which one of Santa's reindeers needs to mind his manners the most?
Rude-olph.

What is red and white and goes up and down and up and down?
Santa Claus stuck in an elevator.

What goes
"Ho, ho, ho,
plop, plop, plop"?
*Santa Claus on
the toilet.*

**This turkey tastes
like an old sofa.**
*Well, you asked for
something with
plenty of stuffing
in it.*

**Who carries all of
Santa's books?**
His books elf.

What does Frosty the Snowman eat for lunch?
Icebergers.

What's red and white and red and white and red and white?
Santa Claus rolling down a hill.

What do sheep say to each other at Christmastime?
"Merry Christmas to ewe!"

Why did the reindeer cross the road?
Because it was tied to a chicken.

Who lives at the North Pole, makes toys, and rides around in a pumpkin?
Cinderelfa!

What goes "Ho, ho, swoosh! Ho, ho, swoosh!"?
Santa stuck in a revolving door.

Why does Santa Claus go down the chimney on Christmas Eve?
Because it soots him.

Where do Frosty the Snowman and his wife go to dance?
Snowballs.

How do you know if there's a reindeer in your refrigerator?
There are hoofprints in the butter.

**Why did the elf sleep
in the fireplace?**
*He wanted to
sleep like a log.*

**How does Mickey
Mouse move around
in the winter?**
On mice skates.

**What can Santa
give away but
still keep?**
A cold.

What did the dog breeder get when she crossed an Irish setter with a pointer at Christmastime?
A pointsetter.

What nationality are Santa and Mrs. Claus?
North Pole-ish.

Elf: Santa, one of the reindeer swallowed my pencil! What should I do?
Santa: Use a pen.

What do you call Frosty the Snowman on Rollerblades?
A snowmobile.

How do you tell the difference between canned turkey and canned custard?
Read the labels.

How does Frosty the Snowman get around?
On an ice-icle.

**My mom bought a huge turkey
for our Christmas dinner.**
That must have cost a fortune!
**Actually, she got it for
a poultry amount.**

**What type of bills do
elves have to pay?**
Jingle bills!

**If Santa Claus
and Mrs. Claus
had a son,
what would
he be called?**
A subordinate clause.

What do you call a chicken at the North Pole?
Lost.

How long should an elf's legs be?
Just long enough to touch the ground!

Who is Frosty the Snowman's favorite aunt?
Aunt Arctica.

23

A boy went into the butcher's shop and saw that the turkeys were 90 cents per pound. He asked the butcher, "Do you raise them yourself?"

"Of course I do," the butcher replied.
"They were only 50¢ a pound this morning!"

Joe: How come you never hear anything about the tenth reindeer, Olive?

Mary: Olive?

Joe: You know—Olive, the other reindeer, used to laugh and call him names . . .

If athletes get athlete's foot, what do elves get?
Mistle-toes.

What did the policeman say when he saw Frosty the Snowman stealing?
"Freeze!"

Who delivers presents to baby crabs?
Sandy Claws!

How does Rudolph know when Christmas is coming?
He looks at his calen-deer.

What type of cake does Frosty the Snowman like?
Any type, as long as it has lots of frosting.

Where does Santa stay when he's on vacation?
At a ho-ho-hotel!

**What does Mrs Claus. sing
to Santa on his birthday?**

*"Freeze a jolly
good fellow!"*

**What makes the turkey
such a fashionable bird?**

*He's always well dressed
for dinner!*

Knock, knock.
Who's there?
Elf.
Elf who?
Elf me wrap this present for Santa!

Knock, knock.
Who's there?
Holly.
Holly who?
Holly up and elf me wrap this present for Santa!

Knock, knock.
Who's there?
Yule.
Yule who?
Yule be sorry if you don't holly up and elf me wrap this present for Santa!

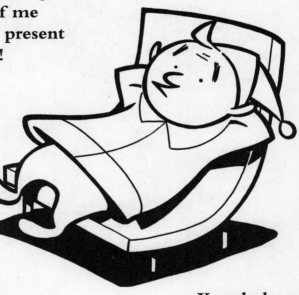

Knock, knock.
Who's there?
Snow.
Snow who?
Snow time to be playing games! Yule be sorry if you don't holly up and elf me wrap this present for Santa!

Mom, can I have a dog for Christmas?
No, you can have turkey
like everybody else.

Why does Santa Claus have a white beard?
So that he can hide
at the North Pole!

Why was the turkey allowed to join the band?
Because it had
the drumsticks.

What do you get if you cross a snowman with a vampire?
Frostbite.

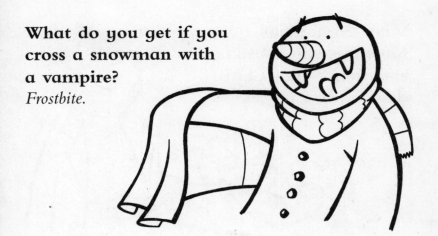

What did the sheep say to the shepherd?
"Season's Bleatings!"

What do you call a wild elf in Texas?
Gnome on the range!

What do you call someone who doesn't believe in Santa Claus?
A rebel without a Claus.

What bird has wings but cannot fly?
A roast turkey.

What do you get when you cross Frosty the Snowman with a baker?
Frosty the Dough-man!

What smells the most in a chimney?
Santa's nose!

What do reindeer have that no other animals on Earth have?
Baby reindeer.

What type of pine has the sharpest needles?
A porcupine.

How do elves greet each other?
"Small world, isn't it?"

What does Santa like to have for breakfast?
Mistle-toast.

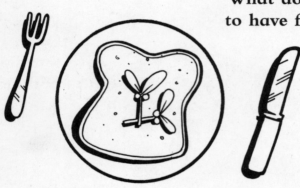

Why does Santa bring presents to children around the world?
Because the presents won't bring themselves!

What do you get if you cross a bell with a skunk?
Jingle smells!

What does Frosty the Snowman drink?
Ice tea.

What's red and green and guides Santa's sleigh?
Rudolph the red-nosed pickle.

Why did the giraffe get a Christmas present?
To thank him for sticking his neck out for everyone.

What did the elf say when he was teaching Santa Claus to use the computer?
"First, yule log in!"

What did the snowman's wife give him when she was mad at him?
The cold shoulder.

How do cows greet each other at Christmastime?
"Mooooory Christmas!"

What does Santa use when he goes fishing?
His north pole!

How do you get into Donner's house?
You ring the deerbell!

What do vampires pour on their turkey on Christmas?
Grave-y.

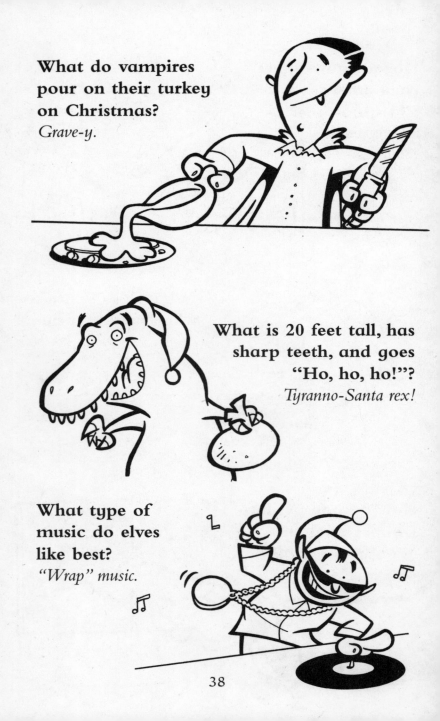

What is 20 feet tall, has sharp teeth, and goes "Ho, ho, ho!"?
Tyranno-Santa rex!

What type of music do elves like best?
"Wrap" music.

How many reindeer does it take to change a lightbulb?
Eight. One to screw in the bulb and the other seven to hold down Rudolph.

What's red and green and flies?
An airsick Santa!

What do you call an elf who steals wrapping paper from the rich and gives it to the poor?
Ribbon Hood.

How did Rudolph learn to read?
He was elf-taught.

Where does Frosty the Snowman keep his money?
In a snowbank.

Why was Santa's little helper depressed?
He had low elf-esteem.

**Where does
Santa Claus
go to vote?**
The North Poll.

**Why do elves scratch
themselves?**
*Because they're the
only ones who know
where they're itchy!*

**What type of
motorcycle does
Santa Claus ride?**
A Holly Davidson.

What do you call Santa Claus after he has come down the chimney?
Cinder Claus!

Why does Santa Claus owe everything to the elves?
Because he is an elf-made man!

What does Frosty the Snowman call ice?
Skid stuff.

What's red and white and gives presents to gazelles?
Santelope.

What does Frosty the Snowman like to put on his icebergers?
Chilly sauce.

What goes "Oh, oh, oh?"
Santa Claus walking backward!

Who sings
"Love Me
Tender" and
makes Christmas
toys?
Santa's little Elvis.

What does Santa
get if he's stuck
in a chimney?
Claustrophobic!

What does Frosty
the Snowman take
when he gets sick?
A chill pill.

What did the bald man say when he got a comb for Christmas?
Thanks. I'll never part with it!

What do you call an elf who tells silly jokes?
A Christmas card!

Who delivers Christmas presents to dogs?
Santa Paws!

If I'm standing at the North Pole, facing the South Pole, and the east is on my left-hand side, what's on my right hand?
Fingers!

What did Adam tell his girlfriend on December 24th?
It's Christmas, Eve.

What's the difference between the Christmas alphabet and the ordinary alphabet?
No "L" (Noel).

What does Tarzan sing at Christmastime?
"Jungle Bells."

How do you make a fool laugh on New Year's Eve?
Tell him a joke on Christmas day.

What is Santa's favorite cereal?
Frosted Flakes.

Do you know that all of the angels in the heavenly choir have the same name?

Sure. Haven't you ever heard the song "Hark, the Harold Angels Sing"?

What did the Japanese tourist wear at the North Pole?

An Eskimono.

Mother: I know you're disappointed with your present, Billy. But, remember, it's the thought that counts.

Billy: Couldn't you have thought a little bigger?

Where did the mistletoe go to become rich and famous?
Hollywood.

What do elves learn in school?
The elf-abet.

David: Have you bought your grandmother's Christmas present yet, Susie?

Susie: No. I was going to get her a handkerchief, but I changed my mind.

David: Why?

Susie: I can't figure out what size her nose is.

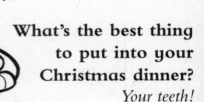

What's the best thing to put into your Christmas dinner?

Your teeth!

Why did the gingerbread man go to the doctor?

Because he was feeling crummy!

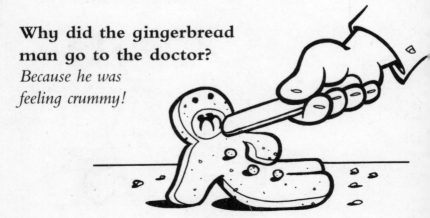

Where is the best place to put your Christmas tree?

Between your Christmas two and your Christmas four!

Knock, knock.
Who's there?
Mary.
Mary who?
Merry Christmas!

**Why do people cry
at Christmastime?**
*Because they get
Santa-mental.*

**What do you get
if you cross an
apple with a
Christmas tree?**
A pine-apple!

**What do you have
in December that
you don't have in
any other month?**
The letter "D."

**Doctor, doctor, help!
I've swallowed some
Christmas decorations.**
*Yes, I can see that you have
a touch of tinselitis.*

Knock, knock.
Who's there?
Doughnut.
Doughnut who?
**Doughnut open
until Christmas!**

Why is it so cold on Christmas?
Because it's in Decembrrrrr!

Why do mummies like Christmas so much?
Because of all the wrapping!

Knock, knock.
Who's there?
Holly.
Holly who?
Holly days are here again!

What type of money do they use at the North Pole?
Cold cash.

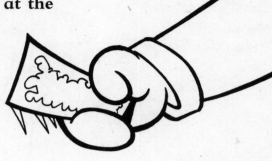

Why should Christmas dinner always be well-done?
So you can say "Merry Crispness!"

Knock, knock.
Who's there?
Wayne.
Wayne who?
Wayne in a manger.

What did one angle say to the other angel?
"Halo there!"

What falls down all the time at the North Pole but never hurts itself?
Snow!

What's red, white, and blue at Christmastime?
A sad candy cane.

There once was a Viking named Rudolph the Red. He was at home one day with his wife. He looked out the window and said, "Look, darling. It's raining."

She shook her head. "I don't think so, dear. I think it's snowing."

But Rudolph knew better, so he said, "Let's go outside, and we'll find out."

They went outside and discovered that, in fact, it was raining. So Rudolph turned to his wife and said, "I knew it was raining. Rudolph the Red knows rain, dear!"

What Christmas carol is popular in the desert?
"O Camel Ye Faithful."

Knock, knock.
Who's there?
Wenceslas.
Wenceslas who?
Wenceslas bus home on Christmas Eve?

Why is it difficult to keep a secret at the North Pole?
Because your teeth chatter.

What does a nearsighted gingerbread man use for eyes?
Contact raisins.

What do you call a letter that is sent up the chimney on Christmas Eve?
Blackmail!

What do angry mice send each other for the holidays?
Crossmouse cards.

"Thanks for the electric guitar you gave me for Christmas," Timmy said to his uncle. "It's the best present I've ever gotten."

"That's great," said his uncle. "Do you know how to play it?"

"Oh, I don't play it. My mom gives me a dollar a day not to play it during the day, and my dad gives me five dollars a week not to play it at night!"

Why did Frosty the Snowman go to live in the middle of the ocean?
Because snowman is an island . . .

How do sheep in Mexico say "Merry Christmas"?
"Fleece Navidad!"

Who works in a department store selling perfume at Christmastime?
Frank Incense.

What was so good about the neurotic doll that Jenny got for Christmas?
It was wound up already.

What do you get if you deep-fry Santa Claus?
Crisp Cringle.

What do reindeer hang on their Christmas trees?
Hornaments.

What type of ball doesn't bounce?
A snowball.

What do you call a bunch of chess champions who are bragging about their games in a hotel lobby?
Chess nuts boasting in an open foyer!

What's the best thing to give your parents for Christmas?
A list of everything you want.

Other titles in the *Sidesplitters*
series you might enjoy: